MW00354112

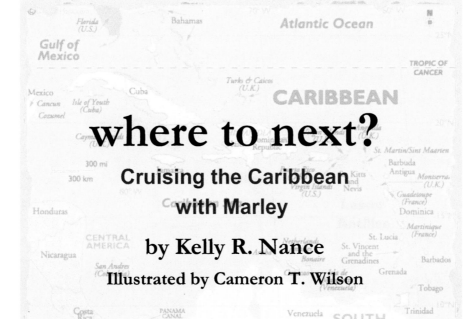

where to next?
Cruising the Caribbean with Marley

by Kelly R. Nance

Illustrated by Cameron T. Wilson

ISBN: 978-0-9994682-2-7

Irie Press

c/o LEADright
50 Sunset Avenue NW
#92383
Atlanta, Georgia 30314
MarleysBook@gmail.com

Visit www.WhereToNextBooks.com

Printed in the United States of America

For more information, please visit *www.WhereToNextBooks.com* or contact
the publisher at MarleysBook@gmail.com.

FOREWORD:

I really like the word destination. Maybe because it sounds like destiny and nation - like setting out in search of a new frontier. But maybe the journey is not at all about finally arriving at some place. No matter how experienced a traveler I have been, I almost always feel like I'm just getting started when it comes to travel. I've never really gotten over feeling like I'm new in most places I visit - even if it's not the first time visiting. And I love that feeling. There's a lot to be said for planning, but some of my best adventures have been when I have thrown away all expectations for a plan and just enjoyed the journey. Wherever you go, be like Marley: enjoy the trip, make new friends, and always try to leave a place better than you found it.

~Michelle Pearcy
Travel Journalist and Photographer
(and good friend of Marley's)

Marley is an adventurous pup who voyages around the world in a backpack. It's Izzy's backpack and she takes it every time she goes with her parents on exciting trips. Izzy's Mom is a travel journalist; and Dad is an environmental scientist. Because both of them travel for work, Izzy is always introduced to interesting destinations with amazing activities that keep her from getting bored.

Together, the family teaches us about the world one trip at a time by exploring

- local food
- architecture
- traditions
- museums
- cultures
- customs
- languages
- transit system
- natural wonde
- historic landmark
- special events
  and so much more!

Through the *Where to Next?* series of travel journeys, children get a glimpse of the wondrous things to see in the world. Hopefully it inspires parents to encourage global minds by taking their children to see some of the places experienced by Izzy and Marley - AND EVEN BEYOND.

(Marley's special words and places appear in blue.)

AUTHOR'S NOTE:

Marley actually cruised the Southern Caribbean in August 2017 - right before two hurricanes devastated its many islands. A portion of the sales from *Where to Next? Cruising the Caribbean* will go toward relief efforts to restore, recover and rebuild them so the islanders can welcome visitors back as soon and safely as possible.

SPECIAL THANKS to my editor and fact-checker 'Cookie Maudress'

> There are no foreign lands. It is the
> traveler only who is foreign.
> ~ Robert Louis Stevenson

Mom and Dad both have work to do in the West Indies on two different Caribbean islands.

Dad is speaking on one island about preserving the Caribbean's natural wonders. On another island, Mom has a workshop about ways people can help the environment while on vacation.

The best way for Mom and Dad to get to both islands is by **Cruising the Caribbean.** When people travel by cruise, they visit different places on a big ship.

Cruise ships are like giant cities floating on water with many fun activities. Cruising is a great way to meet people from all over the world.

Dad, Mom and Izzy will take a special nature cruise that stops at four Caribbean islands. The Caribbean region is made up of the Caribbean Sea and more than 7,000 islands. It is a magical place of history, beaches and sunshine, with plenty native plant and animal life called flora and fauna.

Before people from other countries settled in the Caribbean, Indian tribes like the Taino, Carib, Kalinagos and Arawak lived there. Today, the islands have a blend of Native Indian, African and European cultures.

Izzy searches the internet for exciting things to do when **Cruising the Caribbean**. She finds activities to do onboard the ship, plus fun things about each island.

There are lots of awesome happenings on a cruise ship, and even more at each port of call (where the ship parks). It is smart to plan in advance.

CRUISING ACTIVITIES

on the ship	on the islands
dancing	beach
theme parties	snorkeling
karaoke	rain forest
pajama party	water falls
tea time	site seeing
scavenger hunt	museums
food sculpture	parasail
ice cream social	sea shells
crafts	hiking

Izzy makes a special activity sheet for the trip. She can write in more as they go along.

When **Cruising the Caribbean**, it is important to be prepared for activities. Izzy makes sure to pack:

- ✓ flip flops
- ✓ beach toys
- ✓ snorkel gear
- ✓ sun glasses
- ✓ sun screen
- ✓ camera
- ✓ beach towel
- ✓ hiking sandals

Of course she can't forget Marley!

Mom, Dad and Izzy board the huge ship and find their cabin (room on the ship).

They check out the rest of the ship, meet some of the crew, and get ready to join a big celebration called a Bon Voyage party. This means 'happy voyage.'

Izzy will spend a lot of time at the Kid Sea Camp
– a cool hangout for young folks.
It doesn't take long for her to make a new friend. His
name is Israel but everyone calls him 'Izzy' too.

Israel is cruising with his parents who are from one of
the islands where the cruise ship will go.

The ship's horn blows long and loud to let everyone know it is about to sail (leave the dock). It also means it's time for the Bon Voyage party. It is a Mexican fiesta theme with colorful decorations, piñatas, maracas, a cool photo booth, and plenty Mexican food. Izzy and Israel sample tacos, enchiladas, and tamales.

A Mariachi band plays while they learn salsa, bachata and Calypso dances.

Before bed, everyone enjoys a beautiful sunset at sea. Izzy had so much fun at the fiesta that she asks when they plan to visit Mexico.

In the morning, the ship will dock (arrive) at its first port of call on the beautiful twin islands of St Kitts and Nevis.

St. Kitts and Nevis are two sides of one island. Everyone leaves the ship to begin an island adventure. Israel gets photo-bombed by a funny little monkey. They are Vervet monkeys and can be seen all over the island.

FUN FACT: St. Kitts was named after St. Christopher - the saint of travelers.

They head to Brimstone National Park and climb a ramp of steps to a museum where Dad talks about cultural and natural areas around the world known as World Heritage Sites. These are places with special protection so that their beauty and heritage can be enjoyed for years and years.

Brimstone is the protected site for St. Kitts and Nevis.

One more stop at the top of a steep hill for beautiful views of other islands nearby. Israel meets more interesting animals.

On the way back to the ship, they pass through small villages and farms. While riding up a slope called Monkey Hill they spot more funny furry creatures peeking from the mountains.

Izzy and Israel made a fun game to see who can spot the most monkeys.

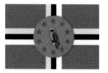 The next port of call is on the island of Dominica. People call it Nature Island because it has three national parks that protect its tropical forests, coral reefs, wetlands and rare colorful parrots.

Israel's Dad drives everyone around to see Dominica's World Heritage Site called Morne Trois Pitons - or Mountain of Three Peaks. He points out pretty

 plants, and pulls over for everyone to sample fruit right off the trees.

They stop in Carib Territory to visit the Kalinago Indians – one of the first tribes to live on Dominica. There is singing, dancing, cassava bread baking, basket weaving and craft making.

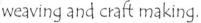

The group also gets to watch as the Kalinago carve the trunk of a tree into a canoe.

*FUN FACT: MABRIKA! is a Kalinaga word that means **WELCOME**!*

Israel's family lives in the capital city. Everyone there is preparing for the island festival called Mas Dominik. This is a big parade with calypso and steel pan music.

Israel's aunt makes dresses and costumes for the children's pageant. She hands Izzy some colorful fabric for her to help. Afterward, Aunt-T let Izzy keep one of the dresses.

While **Cruising the Caribbean**, Sea Days are for everyone to stay onboard the ship while it makes its way to the next stop. Izzy and Israel are busy all day at Kid Sea Camp for kid yoga, shell crafts and an ice cream social.
Another fun activity is the people scavenger hunt.

Kid Sea Camp Scavenger Hunt

Search around the ship for people who fit the descriptions below.

family reunion t-shirt__Meagan____

eating pizza__Mr. Harris____

lives in Canada __De'ja____

sun glasses__Daryl____

blue hat__Alexandria____

first time cruiser__Amanda____

Hawaiian shirt__Asia____

taking a selfie__Emmanuel____

snorkel mask__Dr. Rock____

Later, on the ship, an island carnival theme party begins. Izzy can't wait to wear the costume she helped Aunt-T make. While **Cruising the Caribbean**, she learns about how islanders celebrate Carnival. Just like Mas Dominik in Dominica, everyone wears fancy costumes and dance in the streets. Plus there are pageants, floats, parades, local food, contests and musical bands.

Carnival season may be different for each island, but they all carry deep roots in African traditions.

The plan for the island of St. Lucia is a ride along the countryside, then a day at the beach. After a short drive over twisty roads and crazy hills, they come out of the rainforest and see two mountains that look like cones rising out of the sea. These are The Pitons (peaks) - St. Lucia's World Heritage Site. It has great views for a selfie!

Next, they stop at a public market where Izzy samples local food like homemade bread and banana ketchup.

They also visit the island's famous wood art gallery where everything is made by hand right in the workshop. A sculptor is in the studio hard at work.

TIME FOR *SNUBA!*

Snuba is a mix of snorkeling and scuba diving. Israel shows
Izzy how to use the mask to stay in the water longer.
Under water, they see all kinds of marine life like colorful
fish, sea urchins, star fish, lobsters and coral.

 Jamaica is the last port of call for **Cruising the Caribbean**. The Blue and John Crow Mountains are World Heritage Sites that cover three mountain ranges. Another protected site is Port Royal, which is an underwater city known as the pirate capital.

A friendly islander named Orange takes them to the place where Mom speaks about Volun-tourism. This is a way that people can enjoy traveling while having fun working for a good cause.

Later Orange shows them around magical places on the island including the caves at Roaring River Park.

He leads them through a bunch of tunnels and down steep steps into a cave below. Even though it is dark, you can see natural carvings of animal and human shapes on the walls and ceiling. Each time Orange moves his flashlight to a different spot, another image appears.

Next is a ride through the villages of Fern Gully then through the jungle to a hidden river in the rainforest known as the Blue Hole. People are floating around on inflatable tubes, jumping into the water from high points, and paddling down the lagoon in kayaks.

Cruising the Caribbean is almost over! On the last day aboard the ship, Izzy is super excited to...

...have Tea-Time with mom,

...and play Putt-Putt golf with Dad.

Plus Izzy joins Israel and her other new friends at a pizza party. Then they all watch outdoor movies with yummy popcorn by the pool.

Now back at home, Dad and Izzy enjoy looking through pictures of them **Cruising the Caribbean**.
After every trip, he asks about her favorite part.
Izzy liked everything!

But her **most** favorite parts were all the fun water activities, helping make carnival costumes, meeting people from all over the world, and the delicious banana ketchup.

As Izzy drifts off to sleep she recalls all the amazing places she saw while **Cruising the Caribbean**. She is curious about the next journey.

Follow Izzy and Marley at
www.WhereToNextBooks.com

Other books in the series of

- Springtime in Washington DC
- Visit to New York City
- Road Trip
- *plus more are coming!*

Made in the USA
Middletown, DE
27 December 2022

20477550R00020